D1000270

TRIP IN A BALLOON

du
RT
P
et
R

ALBERT LAMORISSE
Author of "The Red Balloon"

TRIP IN A BALLOON

The photographs in this book were taken while making the film "Trip in a Balloon" by Claude Lamorisse and Alain Duparc

Translated by Malcolm Barnes

DOUBLEDAY & COMPANY, INC.
GARDEN CITY, NEW YORK

LIBRARY OF CONGRESS CATALOG CARD NUMBER 61-7156

Everything was ready. But when Pascal arrived with his suitcase and parrot, his grandfather stopped him and said: "No, Pascal, I can't take you." — "But grandfather," Pascal replied, "you promised me! You always said that your balloon was so easy to handle that even I could steer it." — "Yes," said his grandfather, "but this is an experiment, and I don't know if I've thought of everything. Listen, you can follow in the car with Antoine."

But Pascal, who had dreamed for so long of making the first flight with his grandfather, the inventor, didn't like that plan very much.

CREDIT DU NORD

Then grandfather shouted: " Cast off ! " and the balloon rose into the sky.

Pascal had taken advantage of the excitement of the start to hang on to a sandbag and took off with the balloon. It was neither comfortable nor reassuring, so he closed his eyes. When he opened them again the people and the houses were already very small.

Grandfather glanced at his instruments.

The needle of the altimeter was rising steadily, but too slowly. " Maybe we're too heavy, " he said to himself, when suddenly he saw a panic-stricken hand appear over the edge of the basket.

He seized Pascal, pulled him into the basket, and stood for a moment unable to speak, he was so shaken. What a fall Pascal might have had !

It must not be thought that grandfather's balloon was like other balloons. It didn't just drift; it could be steered. As its inventor had explained when he demonstrated the model to the Aeronauts' Club, this was a balloon that could ascend, descend and be steered, and was, above all, economical, for it was filled with natural air, ordinary air, the kind one breathes.

This was a unique idea, one which was certain to revolutionize existing means of transport.

Grandfather had fitted a car with an apparatus for inflating the balloon. This apparatus reduced the density of the air by passing it through a depressurizing coil, then into a cylinder where it was stabilized, and then into the balloon.

Antoine had been given instructions about where to prepare the landing-places and how to make them visible from the balloon. He had also been told how to set up their camp for the night. All the gear was stowed away in the back of the car and Antoine set off at top speed.

To carry out these orders Antoine had to arrive at the rendezvous first, but for the moment he could scarcely keep up with the balloon. He didn't even have time to stop for lunch. But he had worked out a system of feeding himself whenever he liked without falling behind. He fixed his bottle of wine in a clip, and a long loaf stretched across the windscreen, where he could eat it without taking his hands from the wheel.

Until now Pascal's grandfather and his friends at the Aeronauts' Club seemed to him out-of-date people, who were not living in the present. For him this dream of making progress by going back to the past had seemed completely absurd. But now he was beginning to think that grandfather had indeed invented the perfect means of travel.

Meanwhile Antoine sped along the roads in the direction of the rendezvous.

As for Pascal and his grandfather, they could eat their lunch when they pleased. Naturally Pascal had patched things up with his grandfather. After all, the old man thought, this trip would be a magnificent geography lesson for his grandson.

Already he was dreaming of teachers floating along in balloons with their pupils, explaining to them the formation of deltas, the conditions of life in the valleys, the bareness of the high plateaus, the way the alpine foldings occurred and the movement of glaciers. The pupils would be surprised to notice how from a certain height man appeared to be an artistic animal, a creature both organized and wise. It seemed that in ploughing, planting and harvesting, he had only one idea, to cover the earth lovingly with a fine coat, made of many different pieces of cloth, some rough and some smooth, some shining and some dull, of strange and contrasting colors, some dark and some gay, but all of them pretty.

Grandfather had brought a cold chicken for their lunch, and Pascal ate a leg of it, which he held in both hands as they floated over the fields and villages of France.

When evening fell Antoine had arrived first after all, for the travelers had made a big detour in order to see the Vosges mountains and their fir-trees, as well as Alsace and its storks.

The camp was ready for their arrival.

They ran into difficulties when they landed, because Antoine, though he was willing enough, did not understand much about the handling of balloons. When Pascal got out, the balloon went up again a little and grandfather found himself in an awkward position.

But in spite of it all, grandfather could write in his log-book that this first day had gone according to plan and the balloon had behaved perfectly.

Pascal and Antoine had a game together by lamplight.

When they woke the next morning they were surrounded by a crowd of children, who had come from a nearby summer camp, attracted by the great ball swinging above the bank of the lake. Everything interested the children: the car with its pump, the parrot, the basket and its sandbags, the steering instruments and the compass, the telescope, the altimeter, and the four trumpets that were spouting smoke.

They would all have liked to have gone on the trip. They asked Pascal for his autograph, but he did not know what this was and said to his grandfather: "They're crazy! They're asking me for orthographs. What do they mean?"

When the balloon flew off, the children ran behind it for a long time.

Everything was going well on board. The wind was favorable, and they would soon be in Paris. The members of the Aeronauts' Club must be already watching from their balcony.

The balloon arrived over Paris and came down almost into the streets. At this the Aeronauts' Club was filled with enthusiasm. Even the most sceptical would now believe in it. What a revolution !

This meant the return of the lighter-than-air machines and the end of the noisy ones; it was the rebirth of the balloon. Any man would be able to fly around peacefully and noiselessly in the fresh air with his family.

Taking a risk, grandfather brought the balloon close to the Aeronauts' balcony to show the easy handling of the machine. But he refrained from landing on their roof, as he had intended, because there were too many television aerials. In the future something would be done about the roofs, but the moment for attempting difficult landings had not yet come !

The pre-arranged route had to be followed. After he had received encouragement from his friends at the club, they waved goodbye, and grandfather set his course for the Loire.

Pascal and his grandfather were flying over a forest when suddenly a tree sprang up. But it wasn't a tree; it was a stag! His antlers were so wide that he looked like a bush without any leaves, but running. The stag had been hiding quite motionless in the brush to try to shake off a pack of hounds which had been chasing him for hours. This was not the first time such a thing had happened to him, but this day's ordeal had been a hard one. All morning he had tried every trick he knew, but in vain; the hounds had not lost his scent and the hunting horn had drawn nearer and nearer. And then, when he had found a good hiding place at last, this extraordinary bird had driven him out.

Pascal was thoroughly excited. He wanted to follow the stag and save it. But grandfather was not very keen on that, for the animal kept twisting and turning and they would have to fly in zigzags which might endanger the working of the instruments.

The dogs had spotted their victim once more when they caught sight of the balloonists. They too were seized with fright. But the hunters put them on the trail again. They soon realized that this balloon was trying to save the stag, but in doing so was showing them where the animal was. Things looked bad for the poor stag, who was desperately trying to shake off his pursuers.

Pascal begged his grandfather to do something. The stag was becoming confused and sought refuge in a pond. The horsemen at once rode round the pond to attack the stag when it came out.

But Pascal, seeing what they meant to do, shouted to the stag: " Stop ! You can escape over there ! " The stag heard the advice and turned that way, while grandfather swept down on the dogs and horsemen, sounding the balloon's horn loudly in order to scatter them.

So the stag escaped from the hunters once more and raced away to join his friends in the forest.

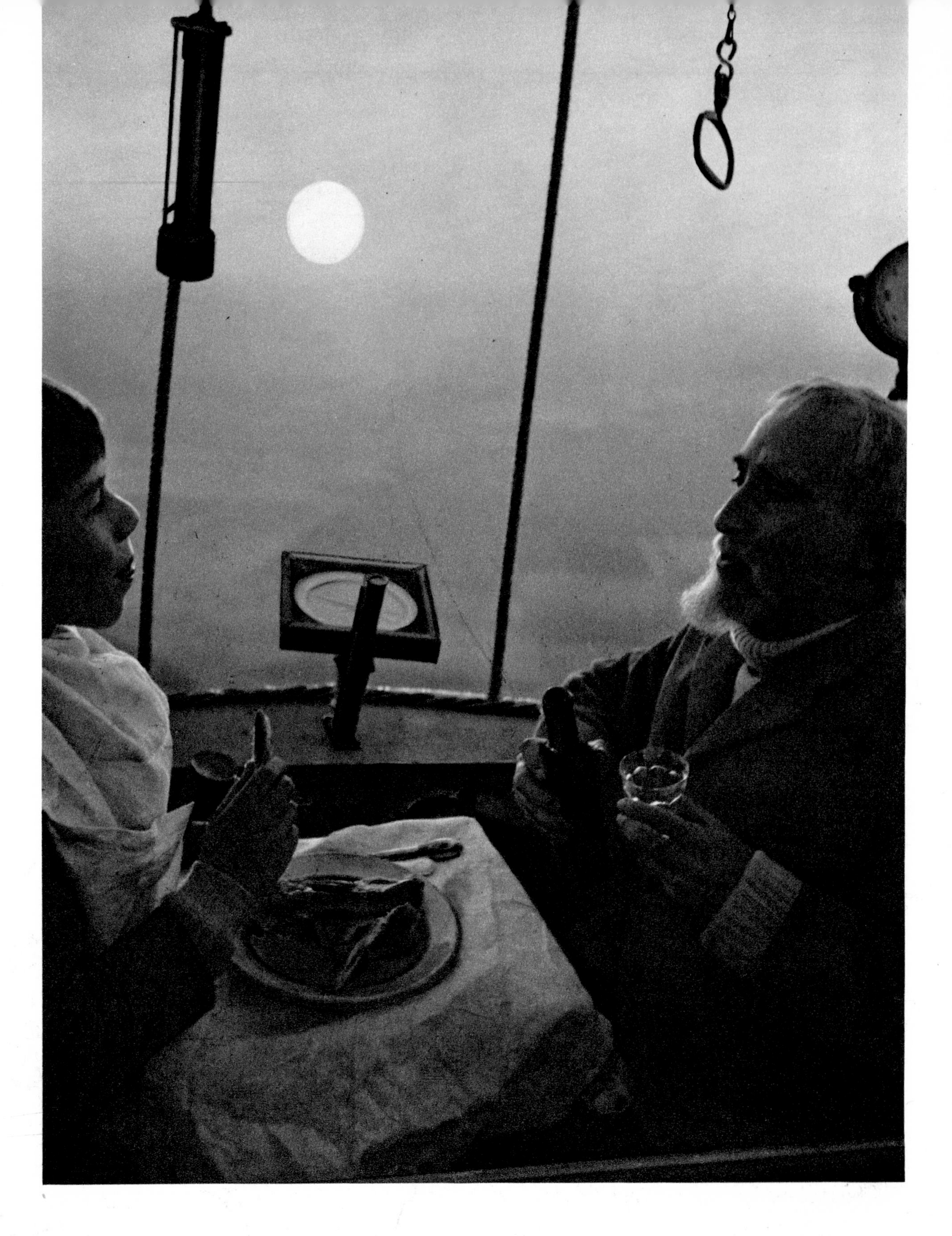

It was part of their plan not to land at all that evening, but to spend the night in the sky. The earth grew quite dark, but the sunlight still fell upon the basket as it hung beneath the balloon in the evening sky. Pascal and his grandfather had their supper and felt very satisfied with their day.

The next morning they woke over the sea. Grandfather was rather surprised at this, but he was able to get his bearings and reach the coast of Brittany. A wedding party hailed them joyfully and invited them down. Grandfather landed the balloon. Everyone was happy. They danced and they had plenty to drink. Meanwhile Antoine had joined them, but he took it into his head to invite a young girl to get into the basket. Then something went wrong and the balloon broke free and went up with the young girl, while Antoine himself hung on to the rope.

The girl was in a tight spot, as you can imagine ! But below her Antoine was holding on tightly and, thanks to his weight, the balloon came down again. Then the rope got away from him ! ..... He caught it again by chasing it on a bicycle, only to be dragged into a pond, and then from one tall rock to another, until finally he was able to fasten the rope.

Grandfather set off again and they flew over the sea once more. Through his telescope he caught sight of a sailing ship all sparkling in the sun.

" Ballon to port ! " cried the look-out. " Baleine ? " (" whale ") cried the captain. " Harpoons ! " — " No, no, a balloon. In the sky ! "

At the Aeronauts' Club they were having a wonderful game with the model that grandfather had left behind after his lecture.

The old aeronauts made it fly in every direction across the room. Suddenly it made an unusual noise, exploded and caught fire.

In consternation they realised that if the model exploded, the balloon would probably do so too, and they were terrified at the thought of the danger into which their friend and his grandson were running somewhere far away in the heart of France.

Meanwhile grandfather was continuing his journey very calmly. Over Auvergne he was suddenly alarmed by a strange hissing sound and prudently decided to land. It was a good thing he did, for just as the basket touched the ground, the balloon caught fire. Pascal could feel the heat of the flames. It was like an exploding sun.

After some feverish research, the Aeronauts decided that the explosion was a case of the well-known Kabinsky phenomenon, upon which neither grandfather nor anyone else had reckoned. Some of them, who had always been a little jealous of grandfather, exclaimed: " You see ! This invention is clearly worthless. " The older members realized that with it would disappear their chances of traveling once more through the skies of their youth. The more practical ones notified the police, so that they might warn grandfather of the danger.

Meanwhile the victims of the accident were making their way to the rendezvous in a cart. Grandfather was working out the causes of the explosion. According to him, it was the effect of static electricity, which in all probability could happen only once in ten thousand times.

Mathematically, therefore, there was no further risk for another ten thousand landings. As Antoine's car contained a spare balloon and since none of the instruments had been damaged, grandfather decided to set off again at once.

And so it was that he took off, without knowing the dangers which threatened him, in the direction of Mont Blanc. A flight over this great peak, he thought, would crown his trip beyond dispute.

They were soon over the mountains. As the temperature fell, so the compression increased, and the strange hissings could be heard once more. But here there was nowhere to land ! Pascal was growing anxious and watching the balloon to see if it was going to explode again. Fortunately, he noticed a leak through which the air was escaping instead of passing through the exhaust tubes.

Even though they were at 13,000 feet above sea level, grandfather felt he had to climb into the rigging to stop the leak. A really wonderful leak it was, too; for it had saved them by preventing the balloon from exploding, though they did not know it. That was how they were able to fly over Mont Blanc.

The cold was terrible and they could hear the wind roaring over the rock ridges. But grandfather was happy. What a success ! What a triumph ! This would be a fine tale for his friends at the Aeronauts' Club ! This would put the last of the doubters to flight !

How tiny the houses looked, down in the valley !

During the night which they spent on board, letting themselves be carried gently towards the Mediterranean Sea, grandfather dreamed of perfecting the balloon. Already he could see another, much bigger balloon with a cabin and a balcony, and very comfortable, like a real house among the clouds.

In the morning they woke to the chirping of cicadas and soon they saw the sea. They came down almost to the water and Pascal insisted that he must have a swim. Grandfather was not very enthusiastic. He tied Pascal to a rope and lowered him into the water. But not for long, for as the balloon became lighter it rose and Pascal found himself hanging in the air, kicking like a frog.

Antoine had prepared a landing-place in the square of the village in Provence where the rendezvous had been arranged and while waiting he had gone to watch a bull-fight a few streets away. Bull-fighting looked very simple to Antoine, and wanting to show what he could do, he entered the arena. But he made the mistake of underestimating the difficulties, with the result that he returned to the square at full speed with the bull on his heels.

Seeing this, the people around the basket panicked. They let go of the ropes and the balloon flew off, carrying Pascal with it.

So another chase began. Antoine went as fast as he could, but in vain. Grandfather was desperate, fearing that Pascal was lost. Antoine observed that he should not have taken a child on board for the first flight, but grandfather answered: " If you had not been playing toreador, the child would not be in danger and the experiment jeopardized. "

Pascal himself was delighted. He was able to steer the balloon as he liked, and as he had watched his grandfather carefully, he knew just what to do. He made the balloon go up and he made it come down, and he chased animals.

But reading the map was another matter! Pascal did not understand it and had no idea where he was going.

The balloon flew on, with the car in pursuit.

As they passed an airfield, Antoine noticed some parachutists climbing into their plane. This gave him an idea.

And so a little later Pascal saw a swarm of parachutes opening in the sky around him. Antoine had jumped with the parachutists and was able to grasp the guy-rope. By climbing along this rope he succeeded in reaching the basket. But being tired and hindered by his equipment, which was strange to him, he seized one of the tubes of the steering gear. This broke and he was thrown into the air. Because he fell from a good height, he had time to open his second parachute and was able to land without harm.

But now the steering apparatus was broken and no longer did what Pascal wanted. Blown along by the wind, the balloon sped toward the sea.

Luckily, Pascal was still able to make the balloon go up or down, and he narrowly avoided the rocks along the shore.

The sea was drawing near. Pascal was frightened and decided to land at all costs, so when the basket was close to the ground, he jumped.

Freed of Pascal's weight, the balloon shot into the sky. And very far away, above the sea, it vanished among the clouds.

It was lost forever. But Pascal knew that his grandfather would much prefer to find him, just Pascal alone, than nothing at all. All he would have to do now was to make another balloon !

Printed by the ISTITUTO ITALIANO D'ARTI GRAFICHE BERGAMO (ITALY)